The Great PJ Elf Chase

· A CHRISTMAS EVE TRADITION ·

Written
by
Judy Voigt and Karen LoBello

Illustrated
by
Lorena Soriano

ISBN: 1482724626
ISBN 13: 9781482724622
Library of Congress Control Number: 2013904650
CreateSpace Independent Publishing Platform
North Charleston, South Carolina

*Dedicated to the memory of
our parents, Callista and Ben Taylor,
who encouraged us in all things,
especially catching elves.*

*With a special nod to our nephew, Al,
the most tenacious elf-catcher of all.*

*To our family and friends—your
suggestions and encouragement meant a lot.*

*Thanks, Barry and Rich,
for your love, help and support
...and for reading our story over and over again!*

*And to Nicholas and Matthew
for all of the extra big hugs.*

"Wake up, Jack.
Tonight's Christmas Eve!
I wonder which PJs
the elves will leave."

"If we're good, Santa's elves
might be extra nice.
They do have that list
that they always check twice."

"Remember last year?
We planned every day
to catch Santa's elves,
but they got away."

"Tonight, do you think
we will capture one?"
"Well, all I can say
is they better run!"

"Ben, how do they know
which house is ours?"
"Jack, those elves can find
any house under the stars."

Shhh! The elves have a secret.
Most kids have no clue.
These sprites spy on children
like Ben, Jack…and you!

The elves' crystal ball tells them
which kids are waiting.
They have a good system
that they've been creating.

Baths must be finished—
On this, elves insist.
The head elf keeps track
of who's next on their list.

"Team two—board the sleigh.
Don't waste time on your tricks.
The Smith kids on Bluff Street
need PJs by six!"

And when the elves see
the delivery's a "go,"
that same crystal ball...
Well, it starts to glow.

Elves gear up for action.
Their sleigh is stacked high.
It's packed with pajamas.
They're ready to fly!

The head elf gives orders,
"Now circle the Earth.
Deliver those PJs from
Rome to Fort Worth!

And remember—no chatter.
Sneak to each bathroom door.
Quickly drop the pajamas
right onto the floor.

If you must squeak and giggle,
make sure kids don't hear.
Then get out of there fast.
Just disappear."

Elves jump from their sleigh
in the midst of the flight.
They slide down to houses
on beams made of light.

How do elves secretly
enter the homes?
It's a magical mystery
known just to these gnomes.

Once they are in,
there is work to be done.
They really should hurry,
but they'd rather have fun!

It's way too inviting.
They just can't resist.
Elves mess up kids' rooms,
then get back to their list.

Now the Taylor boys—
that's young Jack and Ben—
They love getting PJs
again and again.

This Christmas Eve gift
is amazing, that's true.
But the boys know what's
coming: Elf hullabaloo!

"Ben, remember when elves
squirted toothpaste around?"
"Yeah, we couldn't believe
the big mess that we found."

Shaving cream on the mirror!
Hair gel in the sink!
Silly antics the elves
seem to do in a blink.

"Jack, who are we kidding?
We need to step up our game.
If we don't catch an elf,
that would be a real shame."

Jack and Ben are determined.
There must be a way.
Can they figure it out
by the end of today?

Their old dog, McGee,
becomes part of the plan.
(You'd think they were tracking
that Gingerbread Man!)

The brothers high-five.
They've hatched a new plot.
Those daredevil elves
are going to get caught!

This year it will work.
They have traps and a net.
The details have made them
break out in a sweat.

They use night-vision goggles,
contraptions galore.
"Oh no! Did the glue spill
on Mom's brand new floor?"

The boys try it all,
'cause they just want to see
who enters their home
without using a key.

Finally! It's bath time!
They've waited all day.
"Are the elves in the house?"
There is no time to play.

"Hurry up," Ben tells Jack.
"Don't mess around.
If you stay in the tub,
those elves won't be found."

McGee is their lookout,
with his rubber sword.
Though, sadly, he looks
just a little bit bored.

Surely he'll bark if there's
something suspicious.
He knows his reward
will be extra delicious.

Jack and Ben hear strange noises.
"The elves must be near.
Get out of the tub, Jack!
Our PJs are here!"

The excitement explodes.
Jack hops out of the bath.
They fling open the door
and start blazing a path.

"**P**Js *and* hats! Hmm...
How'd those elves know?
The cartoon on the front
is from my favorite show!"

"Wow! Look what they did.
This room is a wreck.
Pillows thrown! Lotions dumped!
Crazy elves! What the heck?!"

There's no time to try on
the PJs they got.
The Taylor boys need to
stick to their plot.

"Check trap number one—
There was cheese to be had.
They got it. Oh, brother!
Those elves…They are bad!"

"Oh no…Is it true?
This can't possibly be…
Trap number two's
wrapped around poor McGee!"

Ben's anxious to find them.
His fire's ignited.
He's hot on their trail.
Could he be more excited?

He cinches his towel—
Then takes off for the chase.
Sure, elves are quick,
but Ben's good in a race.

He bounds through the snow.
Those elves will go down!
He tracks all their moves
as if *he's* a hound.

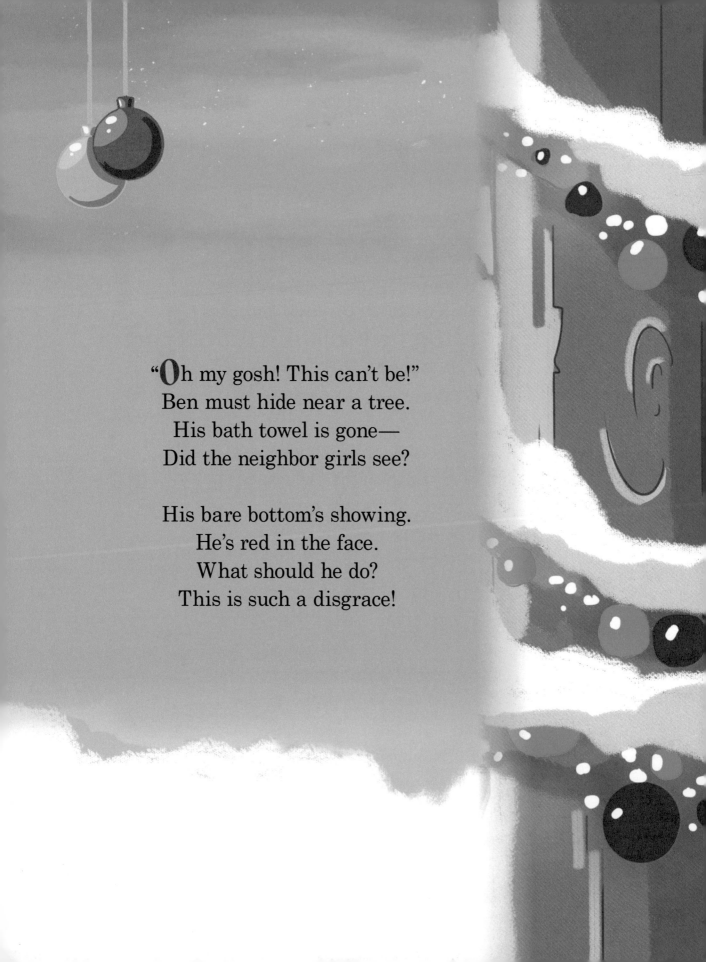

"Oh my gosh! This can't be!"
Ben must hide near a tree.
His bath towel is gone—
Did the neighbor girls see?

His bare bottom's showing.
He's red in the face.
What should he do?
This is such a disgrace!

Jack runs to the rescue.
There was no need to fear.
He's carrying Ben's towel,
with a grin, ear-to-ear.

Ben moans to his brother,
"The elves got away."
"You *almost* caught them"
is what Jack had to say.

"Next year, we'll get them.
They won't stand a chance!
Put our heads together—
Plan way in advance!"

Wagging his tail,
McGee runs toward the boys.
They jump up and high-five,
"Tomorrow—the toys!"

My Page

This Book Belongs to

_____

Now it's time to count the elves.
Start on the front cover and go all the way to the
back cover. How many elves can you find?
Be careful — elves like to hide!

**This is the number of elves I counted in
"The Great PJ Elf Chase" book: _____**

Visit our website to find out
if you were correct!!

www.TheGreatPJElfChase.com